291783
Edwin Loe Elem. School
New Town, N. Dak.

Mrs. Jeepers Is Missing!

3.7

There are more books about the Bailey School Kids!
Have you read these adventures?

#1 Vampires Don't Wear Polka Dots
#2 Leprechauns Don't Play Basketball
#3 Santa Claus Doesn't Mop Floors
#4 Werewolves Don't Go to Summer Camp
#5 Ghosts Don't Eat Potato Chips
#6 Frankenstein Doesn't Plant Petunias
#7 Aliens Don't Wear Braces
#8 Genies Don't Ride Bicycles
#9 Pirates Don't Wear Pink Sunglasses
#10 Witches Don't Do Backflips
#11 Skeletons Don't Play Tubas
#12 Cupid Doesn't Flip Hamburgers
#13 Gremlins Don't Chew Bubble Gum
#14 Monsters Don't Scuba Dive
#15 Zombies Don't Play Soccer
#16 Dracula Doesn't Drink Lemonade
#17 Elves Don't Wear Hard Hats
#18 Martians Don't Take Tempertures
#19 Gargoyles Don't Drive School Buses
#20 Wizards Don't Need Computers
#21 Mummies Don't Coach Softball

Mrs. Jeepers Is Missing!

by Debbie Dadey
and
Marcia Thornton Jones

illustrated by John Steven Gurney

SCHOLASTIC INC.
New York Toronto London Auckland Sydney

If you purchased this book without a cover, you should be aware that this book is stolen property. It was reported as "unsold and destroyed" to the publisher, and neither the author nor the publisher has received any payment for this "stripped book."

No part of this publication may be reproduced in whole or in part, or stored in a retrieval system, or transmitted in any form or by any means, electronic, mechanical, photocopying, recording, or otherwise, without written permission of the publisher. For information regarding permission, write to Scholastic Inc., 555 Broadway, New York, NY 10012.

ISBN 0-590-84885-2

Text copyright © 1996 by Debra S. Dadey and Marcia Thornton Jones
Illustrations copyright © 1996 by Scholastic Inc.
All rights reserved. Published by Scholastic Inc.
LITTLE APPLE PAPERBACKS and the LITTLE APPLE PAPERBACKS logo are trademarks of Scholastic Inc.
THE BAILEY SCHOOL KIDS and THE ADVENTURES OF THE BAILEY SCHOOL KIDS are trademarks of Scholastic Inc.

12 3 4 5 6 7/0

Printed in the U.S.A. 40

First Scholastic printing, July 1996

Book design by Laurie Williams

Contents

To Thelma Thornton because some
of my best memories are of those holiday parties when
you invited all of us monsters to dinners!
— MTJ

For all the kids who went to Weaverton Elementary
School in Henderson, Kentucky and the special
teachers who taught there.
— DD

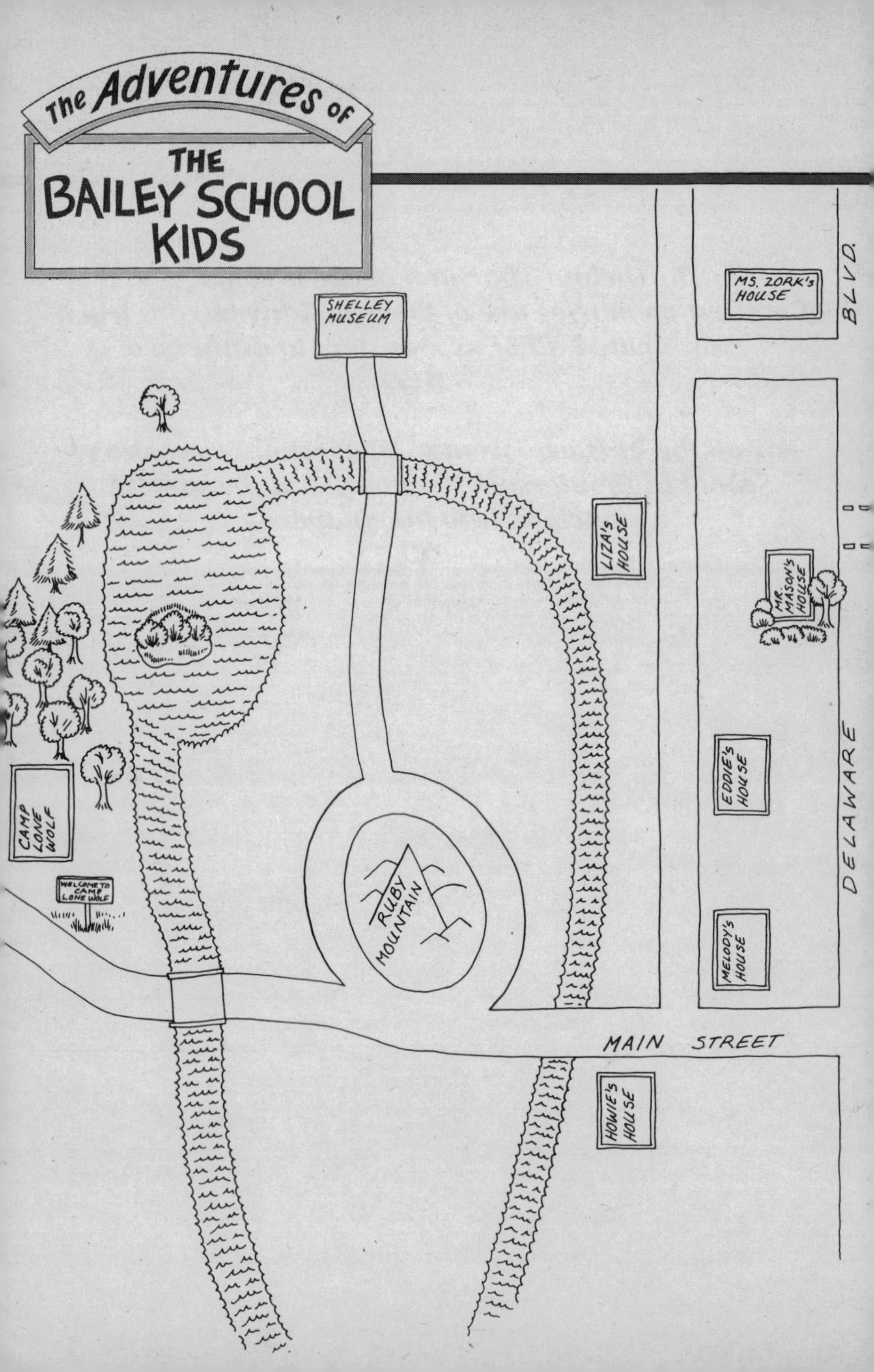
The Adventures of
THE
BAILEY SCHOOL
KIDS
SHELLEY MUSEUM
MS. ZORK'S HOUSE
BLVD.
LIZA'S HOUSE
MR. MASON'S HOUSE
DELAWARE
EDDIE'S HOUSE
CAMP LONE WOLF
WELCOME TO CAMP LONE WOLF
RUBY MOUNTAIN
MELODY'S HOUSE
MAIN STREET
HOWIE'S HOUSE

Welcome to Bailey City!

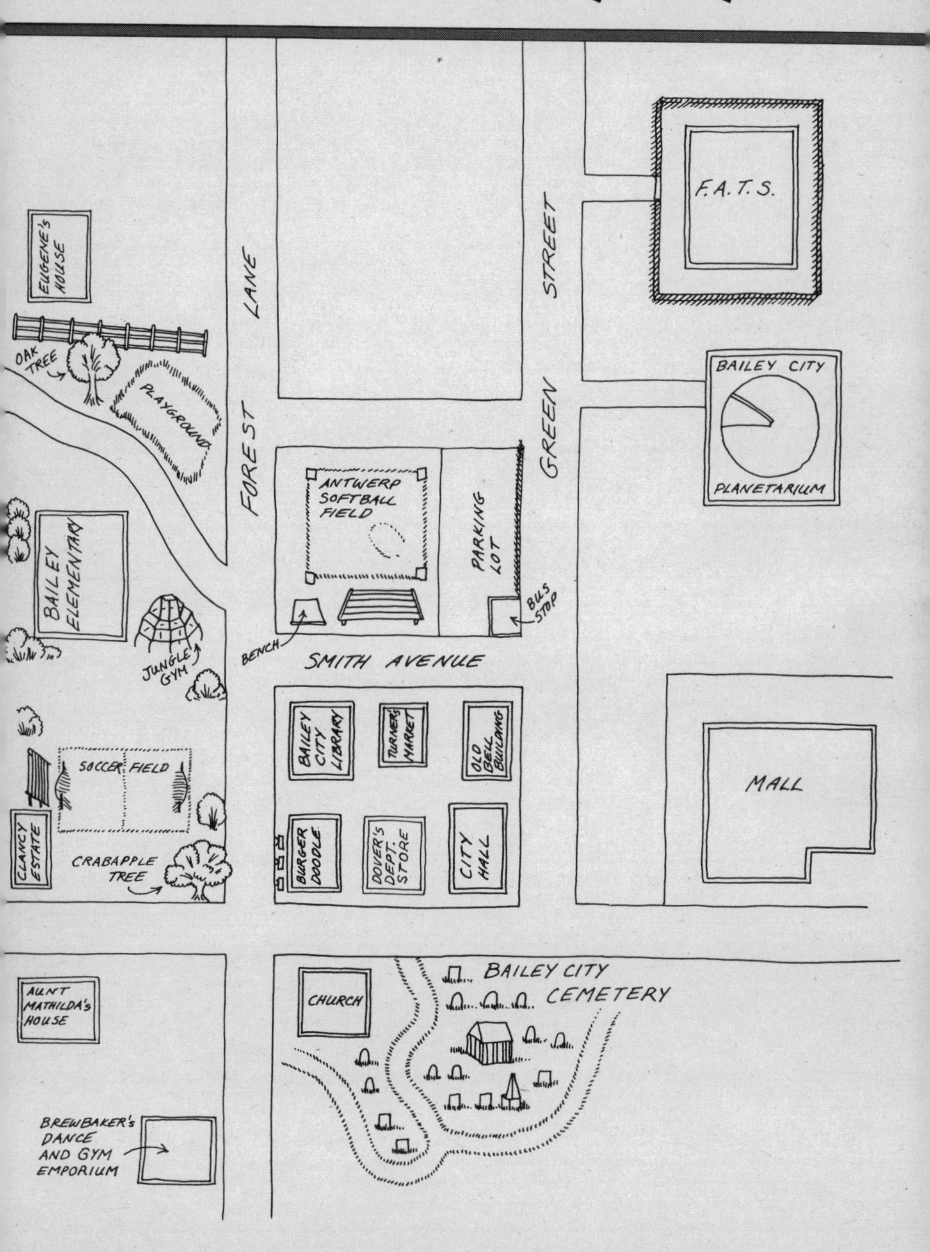

1

BBQ

"This is horrible," Eddie complained. "No one should have to do this."

Liza giggled. "Mrs. Jeepers is being nice by inviting us to this end-of-the-year party. You're acting like she's going to barbecue you for supper."

Liza, Eddie, and their friends, Howie and Melody, stood on the crumbling sidewalk to the old Clancy Estate where their third-grade teacher lived. Most of the kids thought Mrs. Jeepers was a little strange, maybe even a vampire. They were sure the green brooch she always wore had magical powers. Every time she rubbed it, her green eyes flashed and the brooch glowed brighter. It even stopped Eddie from misbehaving too much.

"I say we should go while we still can," Eddie said.

Howie nodded, looking up at the peeling paint on the huge Clancy mansion. Broken shutters hung at lopsided angles, and a branch from a nearby dead oak tree scraped against a cracked window. "We could turn around and leave," Howie said. "Mrs. Jeepers would never know the difference."

"Mrs. Jeepers put up with us for most of the year," Melody reminded them. "It won't hurt us to be nice for a few minutes."

"A vampire teacher sucking my blood dry is sure to hurt a little bit," Eddie argued.

Eddie turned to leave when a girl from their class came through the gate behind them. "Hi, Eddie," Carey squealed, grabbing Eddie's arm. "Isn't this exciting?"

"Yeah," Eddie muttered, "just like watching paint dry."

Carey ignored Eddie and chattered on. "Here we are invited to one of the oldest houses in Bailey City for an evening barbecue and you're a grouch. Come on, I hear some of the other kids."

Carey pulled Eddie around to the back of the house. Melody, Howie, and Liza followed. Huge paper lanterns hung all around the backyard. Cheerful red-and-white tablecloths covered four long tables. Half a dozen kids from their class were already there, playing kickball beside the tables.

"Look at Mrs. Jeepers," Melody said. The five kids stared at their third-grade teacher. Mrs. Jeepers wore her favorite outfit, a purple-and-green-polka-dotted dress with a green brooch. She even had her usual bright green painted fingernails. But a white apron was strapped around her waist and a huge

white chef's hat perched on top of her long red hair. She stood in front of a smoking barbecue grill.

"Oh, great," Eddie muttered. "She's ready to cook us alive."

2

Mush and Brew

"Don't be silly," Liza told Eddie. "You know Mrs. Jeepers isn't really a vampire."

"We don't know that for sure," Eddie said. "But I do know that if I have to be here, I might as well have fun." Eddie and Melody ran off to play kickball. Liza and Howie walked over to say hello to Mrs. Jeepers.

"Thank you for inviting us," Liza told Mrs. Jeepers. "Can we help you?"

Mrs. Jeepers flashed her green eyes at Liza and Howie and spoke in her Romanian accent. "I am delighted you could make it. Would you like to finish preparing the brew?"

"Brew?" asked Howie.

"Yes, Cold Brewbaker's Brew is one of my favorite drinks. Just fill these cups with the brew in that pot." Mrs. Jeepers pointed to a big black cauldron before turning back to the smoking grill.

Howie peered at the foamy orange liquid bubbling near the top of the pot. "Do you think it's safe?" he whispered to Liza.

"Let's get Eddie to try it." Liza giggled. "If he doesn't die, we'll drink it, too." They poured the brew into cups, being careful not to spill any of the foaming liquid on their hands.

As they finished they heard a loud shout. Howie jumped out of the way just in time. The kickball landed right in the pot of leftover Brewbaker Brew. Orange foam flew everywhere. Liza screamed as the foam splashed onto her T-shirt and face.

Eddie came up and grabbed the kickball out of the pot. "Sorry about that," he said with a grin. "Liza, you look like a crazed cantaloupe."

Eddie fell silent when Mrs. Jeepers flashed her eyes in his direction. Eddie mumbled another apology and ran off to kick the ball to Melody.

"Thank you so much," Mrs. Jeepers said from behind them. "You are such a help. Would you like to set out the monster mush and bread? Liza, you may wipe yourself off while you are in the kitchen."

"Monster mush?" Howie and Liza said together.

"It is just inside the kitchen door. You may set one bowl on each table, along with some bread," Mrs. Jeepers told them.

"Next she'll have us scooping out Dracula droppings," Howie whispered.

Liza giggled, but she stopped laughing when she opened the door to Mrs. Jeepers' kitchen.

3

Brains

"It looks like something exploded in here," Howie said.

Liza nodded. "Or someone exploded."

Howie and Liza gulped and looked around the kitchen. A big spiderweb hung from the ceiling and orange goo dripped from the kitchen counter. Dirty bowls were piled high in the sink. Brown slime oozed down the sides of a huge pan on the stove. Red blobs splattered the floor around a chipped wooden table. The table itself was caked with brown and white blobs. Four huge bowls sat on the table along with two loaves of bread.

"This must be the monster mush," Liza said, picking up two of the bowls.

"It looks more like banshee brains to

me," Howie said, holding the bowls as far from his body as possible.

"I think I've lost my appetite," Liza admitted. But when Liza and Howie went out the door, the other kids had already gathered around the long tables. Huge piles of burgers were in the center of each table.

"Eat up," Mrs. Jeepers told them. "I hope you like Double Onion Doodle Burgers."

"I'm so hungry I could eat the spots off a zebra," Eddie said, gulping down a big bite.

Howie laughed and reached for a bowl of garlic chips. "All right," he said, "these are my favorite."

Liza put the monster mush and bread down before sitting next to Melody. "Are you going to eat that stuff?" Liza asked Melody.

Melody nodded her head. "Sure," she said after taking a bite, "it's good. And we'd better eat fast. I think a storm is coming."

Liza looked up. Sure enough, the paper lanterns were swinging in the breeze and clouds churned in the darkening sky. As she took a bite of her burger a big flash of lightning ripped across the sky.

Carey screamed and Mrs. Jeepers stood up from her seat. "Please take your plates into the house. We'll eat in the dining room until this storm passes."

Rain was already falling when the kids stepped inside Mrs. Jeepers' house. Everyone was silent as they stared at the huge cobweb-covered chandelier hanging from the high ceiling. A massive wooden staircase with blood-red carpet led up into the darkness. Cobwebs clung to the walls and a dusty mist filled the air.

"Please eat up," Mrs. Jeepers told them as she ushered the class into the dining room. "I am sure the storm will end

quickly." The kids settled around a large wooden table and began eating. Before long, everyone was chatting about the end of school and summer plans. No one noticed that the storm outside was getting worse. Then suddenly the lights flickered out and everyone screamed.

4

Ghost Story

Liza grabbed Melody's arm and whimpered, "I'm scared."

"Do not worry, children," Mrs. Jeepers said, striking a match above her head. "The storm must have caused us to blow a fuse. I will light some candles so you may finish your food." Mrs. Jeepers went about the foyer and dining room lighting huge candles. Soon there was enough light to see by, but everything took on an eerie glow in the flickering light.

"I'm not so hungry anymore," Howie said. He put his garlic chip back on his plate and shivered. "I'm ready to go home."

"Me, too," Liza said.

Melody looked out a dusty window. "The storm's really terrible out there. I don't think Mrs. Jeepers is going to let us go anywhere until it calms down."

"Then we're trapped," Eddie said softly.

Howie gulped. "Trapped in a haunted house."

Eddie's eyes gleamed in the candlelight. "This is the perfect place to tell a ghost story. And I know just the one."

"I have a feeling that I'm not going to like this," Liza said with a sigh.

"Once upon a time," Eddie started.

"What kind of scary story starts with 'Once upon a time'?" Melody asked.

"The best kind," Eddie said with a frown. "Anyway, there once was this huge old house, kind of like this one, but no one lived there. It was empty except for these really strange pictures on the wall."

"Lots of people have pictures on their walls," Howie said. "There's nothing strange about that."

"Except that these pictures came to

life," Eddie said. "And whenever anyone went into the house, they were never seen again!"

Liza put her hands over her ears. "I don't want to hear anymore. I'll have nightmares."

"Good, you can come with me to the bathroom," Melody said.

"Don't you think it'd be safer to stay here with everyone else?" Liza asked. "It almost looks like a tornado out there."

"I can't help it," Melody said. "I really have to go and Carey told me the bathroom is that way." Melody pointed down a dark hallway.

Liza shook her head. "I don't want to go."

"Fine," Melody said, getting up from the table. "Stay here and listen to Eddie's story."

Liza jumped up. "I have a feeling I'm going to regret this. But, I'm coming."

5

A Very Bad Idea

A streak of lightning lit the long hall, making Liza's and Melody's shadows look like monsters with huge heads. Liza held a candle out in front of her. Her hands shook just a little.

"Eddie was right," Liza said. "We shouldn't have come to this party in the first place."

"You're being silly," Melody told her friend.

"You mean you still think coming here was a good idea?" Liza asked.

Melody shook her head so hard one of her pigtails slapped Liza on the cheek. "No. This was a very bad idea. But you're silly to say Eddie was right. Eddie is never right."

"He was right today," Liza said with a sniffle. "Now we're stuck here."

"We'll leave as soon as the storm lets up," Melody told Liza. She had to almost shout over the noise of thunder rattling the windows.

As they turned the corner another jagged bolt of lightning cut through the dark long enough for Melody and Liza to catch a glimpse of the corridor leading toward the bathroom.

"Did you see that?" Liza whimpered.

"See what?" Melody asked.

"The pictures," Liza whispered. "They're just like the ones in Eddie's story."

"Don't be silly," Melody said. "Lots of people hang pictures in hallways. I bet they're Mrs. Jeepers' aunts and uncles."

Liza held her candle high above her head. "I hope you're wrong," she said softly. "These are not pictures of normal relatives."

Outside, the wind moved the trees and an old branch scratched at a cracked windowpane.

"Let go of my shoulder," Melody hissed.

"I'm not touching your shoulder," Liza said, "I'm holding this candle."

Melody looked at Liza and Liza looked at Melody. Then they both looked down at the strange hand resting on Melody's shoulder.

"Ahhh!" Melody screamed before the strange hand smacked her mouth shut.

6

Gallery of Monsters

"What are you screaming for?" Eddie hissed.

Liza held the candle close to Eddie's and Howie's faces. "You scared us to death," Liza said. "You shouldn't sneak up on people like that."

"And you shouldn't cook my eyeballs for dessert," Eddie warned her, backing away from the candle.

"Besides," Howie added, "we weren't creeping up on you. We just wondered if you've seen Mrs. Jeepers."

"We saw something," Liza said. "But it wasn't Mrs. Jeepers. Look!" She pointed to the pictures lining the hallway. "It's just like in Eddie's story."

Eddie put his nose close to a picture so he could see it. "No," he said softly. "This is worse. Much worse." The four friends peered up at the picture of a man with cold black eyes and an evil grin.

"Look at his teeth," Melody whispered. "They look sharper than scissors."

"And his skin is whiter than milk," Liza added. "He's familiar. I wonder who he is."

"Don't you recognize him?" Howie asked. "It's Mr. Drake."

"MR. DRAKE!" his three friends shouted. Just the mention of their school counselor sent goosebumps skipping up their backs. Most of the Bailey School kids thought Mr. Drake was really Count Dracula.

"Why would Mrs. Jeepers have a picture of our school counselor in her hallway?" Liza asked.

Howie didn't answer. He grabbed Liza's candle and hurried to the next picture. Eddie peered over his shoulder.

"That's Mr. Jenkins," Eddie said, looking at a picture of a very hairy face.

"He's the werewolf that runs Camp Lone Wolf."

The next picture showed a huge giant with scars crisscrossing his cheeks. "That's Frank from the Shelley Museum," Liza whispered. "I'd recognize those scars anywhere."

"You mean the Frankenstein monster from the Shelley Museum," Melody reminded her.

"Why would Mrs. Jeepers have these pictures hanging in her hallway?" Howie asked.

"It's like her very own gallery of monsters," Eddie said.

"What if they come alive like the pictures in Eddie's story?" Liza asked.

"Don't be silly," Melody told her. "I'm sure there's a very good reason for this. Let's just find Mrs. Jeepers and ask her."

Howie shook his head. "We can't."

"Why not?" Melody asked.

"Because," Howie said slowly, "Mrs. Jeepers is missing!"

7

Missing!

"Missing?" Melody asked. "What makes you think she's missing?"

"Because no one has seen her since dinner," Howie said.

"Maybe she's fixing dessert in the kitchen," Liza suggested.

"Nope," Eddie told her. "We looked there."

"Just because she's not in the kitchen doesn't mean she's missing," Liza pointed out.

Eddie grinned. "Liza's right. After all, Mrs. Jeepers is a vampire. Everyone knows vampires hunt for fresh blood when the sun goes down. Maybe she's out looking for a snack."

Melody ignored Eddie. "I'm sure she's just resting."

"I wonder," Eddie said with a giggle, "if Mrs. Jeepers sleeps hanging upside down like a bat."

"We're the batty ones for hanging around this creepy place," Howie said. "We should go home."

"We can't," Melody said. "The storm is terrible, it'd be dangerous to go outside."

"It's dangerous to stay here," Howie said.

"We can't go home now," Liza said. "I'm worried about Mrs. Jeepers. We have to look for her."

Eddie shook his head. "As far as I'm concerned, a missing teacher is the best kind of teacher. I say we get out of here while we can."

"But what if she fell in the dark?" Liza said. "She could be hurt."

"We should make sure she's all right," Melody said.

Eddie glanced at the pictures on the wall. It looked like every painted eyeball stared straight down at him. "None of us may be safe," he warned.

Melody, Liza, and Howie followed Eddie back down the long hallway. Flickering candles met them when they reached the dining room.

The rest of the third-graders huddled in a corner. Tears puddled in Carey's eyes. "I don't like this one bit," she complained. "I tried to call Daddy to come get us, but the phone lines are dead."

"The storm knocked out the phones

along with the electricity," a chubby boy named Huey told them. "We better find Mrs. Jeepers before all her ice cream melts."

"Let's go look for her," Melody suggested.

"Are you crazy?" Carey wailed. "This old house is too spooky to wander around in."

"But we have to find Mrs. Jeepers," Liza told the other third-graders.

"I'm not leaving this corner until the lights come back on," one of the kids muttered.

"Me, neither," most of them said.

"Oh, come on," Liza said. She grabbed an extra candle and faced her three best friends. "I guess we'll have to do it ourselves."

"Are you sure you want to?" Melody asked.

Liza took a deep breath. "We have no choice."

8

The Search

"Follow me," Liza said. She led her friends to the massive wooden staircase in the front hall. Liza gripped the railing and began climbing the steps covered in blood-red carpet with her friends close behind.

Liza paused at the top. "Which way do we go?" she asked. Just then, a door slammed at one end of the long, dark upstairs hallway.

"Mrs. Jeepers?" Melody called. The rumble of thunder and rain drumming on a nearby window was all they heard.

"I think we should go this way," Eddie said, and headed in the other direction.

Howie grabbed his friend's elbow. "We should see what made that door slam," Howie told Eddie.

"Howie's right," Liza said. "Mrs. Jeepers may need us. Follow me."

Slowly, step-by-step, the three friends followed Liza. Melody hung on Liza's shoulder and Howie followed close behind. Eddie kept looking over his shoulder to make sure no monsters followed them.

Liza stopped before a closed door at the end of the hall. She had to hold her candle with both hands to keep it from shaking.

"Go ahead," Melody told her. "Open the door."

"Are you ready?" Liza asked.

"I'm ready," Melody said.

"Me, too," Howie said.

"What about you, Eddie?" Liza asked.

But Eddie didn't answer. Liza, Melody, and Howie slowly turned around.

"Oh, no!" Melody gasped. "He's gone!"

Boo!

"Boo!" A short monster with an incredibly ugly face jumped out from a dark room.

"AAAAH!" Howie, Melody, and Liza screamed.

"Ha! Got you!" Eddie laughed as he took off the mask he was wearing. "You nearly jumped as high as Ruby Mountain!"

"Eddie!" Liza scolded. "You shouldn't scare people like that."

"My heart is still doing somersaults," Howie said.

Melody pointed to the mask in Eddie's hands. "Where did you get that horrible thing?"

Eddie pointed over his shoulder to a dark room. "You won't believe what's in

there." He held his candle high so Melody, Liza, and Howie could see inside the room. A long table was covered with masks of all kinds.

"Why would our third-grade teacher have a room filled with ugly faces?" Liza asked.

"Why not?" Eddie joked. "After all, she spends her school days in a classroom filled with ugly faces. Maybe this reminds her of school."

Melody tried to hide a giggle, but it came out like a snort. "Then that really disgusting one must be you."

Eddie put the mask on. "Very funny," he growled.

"Quit messing around," Liza said.

"Liza's right," Howie said. "Put that mask down. We have to find Mrs. Jeepers."

Eddie shook his head. "I'm wearing this mask. Maybe it will scare away any vampires we run into."

"Good idea," Liza said. "Then you can lead the way."

"I'm not going first," Eddie told her. "This is your idea. You should go first."

"But you have the mask," Liza pointed out. "Or are you chicken?"

"I'm not a chicken," Eddie snapped and went down the hall to the closed door. Outside, the wind blew angrily against the side of the house and rain beat the roof.

"Go ahead," Howie whispered when they were all huddled outside the door. "Open it."

Eddie gripped the door handle. It felt cold in his hand. Slowly he turned the knob, and when the door creaked open, they saw wooden steps leading up to a pitch-black attic.

"Listen," Melody hissed. "There's something up there."

The four kids stood still. Sure enough, they could hear a thumping that sounded

like the beating heart of a monster.

"What do you think it is?" Howie asked.

"Maybe it's Mrs. Jeepers," Liza said. "She might be knocking on the floor to get our attention."

"We'd better find out for sure," Howie said bravely. "Go ahead, Eddie. We're right behind you."

"Gee, thanks," Eddie said. "I feel safer already." But he slowly climbed the steps of the attic.

Thunder growled overhead and a sudden downpour of rain splatting the roof was so loud it almost covered the sound of the steps groaning under their feet. Cobwebs clung to their faces and Eddie saw a mouse skitter out of their way as they climbed higher and higher.

Finally, Eddie's sneaker touched the top step. When he held up his candle to see better, a shadow swooped down, skimming over the top of his head.

"Run!" he yelled. "Run for your lives!"

10

Long Slide Down

The four kids raced down the attic steps, but the quick movement caused their candles to flicker out. It was as black as a witch's cat in the second-floor hallway until a flash of lightning lit up the big first-floor staircase.

"This way!" Eddie screamed. He bounded to the stairway. He didn't bother scrambling down the steps. With one jump, Eddie landed on the stair rail and slid down.

His three friends joined him on the long slide down to the bottom of the steps. "Wheee!" Eddie yelled, until he landed with a *thump* at the bottom of the stairs.

Thump. Thump. Thump. Melody, Howie, and Liza landed in a heap right on top of Eddie.

"OW! Are you trying to kill me?" Eddie complained as the kids stood up.

"No, we were just trying to save our lives," Melody said, straightening her pigtails.

"Do you think that was Mrs. Jeepers flying around up there?" Howie asked. He and Liza picked up the candles and relit them from one of the big candles Mrs. Jeepers had lit earlier. The big candle was already burned halfway down.

"Naw," Eddie said matter-of-factly. "It was probably just one of her bat friends. After all, this place has rats. So, it probably has bats, too."

"Rats?" Liza whimpered.

"Sure," Eddie told her. "All old houses have rats. It's perfectly normal."

"I want to go home," Liza said. She looked ready to cry.

"I thought you wanted to find Mrs. Jeepers," Melody reminded her.

"All I want to do is find my bed and crawl under the covers," Liza said.

"What was that noise?" Howie asked.

"It's just the storm," Melody said. "It's really loud."

Howie shook his head. "I heard something coming from behind that door. It sounded like a crash."

"Maybe it's Mrs. Jeepers," Liza said.

"Let's check," Melody said.

Eddie opened a door beside the big

staircase and stared into the darkness.

"What is it?" Melody asked.

Eddie gulped as he heard another crash coming from below. "It's the basement."

11

The Box

Finally, Liza got the courage to speak. "We have to go down there."

"Don't you remember what's there?" Melody asked. Her friends nodded slowly. They had all seen a long box being carried into their teacher's basement, a long box that looked like a coffin. Eddie and Melody had even tried to open the box. Then they heard sounds coming from inside it. That had been a long time ago, but they had never forgotten how scared they had been.

"A vampire's coffin is down there," Eddie said with certainty. "We can't go down there unless we're crazy."

Howie nodded. "Mrs. Jeepers probably sleeps in there and she's probably resting right now."

Eddie put his hand on Howie's arm. "But it's dark now, that's when vampires are most awake. Mrs. Jeepers may be down there all right. But she may be waiting for us."

"She probably wants us for her dessert," Howie said with a big gulp.

"It's too dangerous," Melody agreed. "I don't think we should take the chance."

"I thought you didn't believe in vampires," Eddie said to Melody.

"You mean you *want* to go down there?" Melody asked.

"Not really," Eddie admitted. "But I'm getting tired of hanging around this joint. I want to get to the bottom of this mess."

"The basement is the bottom," Liza said. "And maybe Mrs. Jeepers is down there. She could need our help."

"After all," Eddie said, more bravely than he felt, "it's just a basement."

"I guess we're all crazy then," Howie said with a sigh. "Let's go."

12

Green and Glowing

The candle light flickered and danced as the kids descended into the drafty basement. The cold darkness seemed to swallow them up and the tiny flames barely gave enough light for them to see the damp steps.

"We are definitely crazy for doing this," Howie complained. "Couldn't we just go hide in the corner like everyone else?"

"Carey and those kids are just a bunch of babies," Eddie said as he peered into the darkness. "At least we have some guts."

Melody gulped. "I'd like to keep my guts exactly where they are. I don't want any monster getting hold of them."

"Don't be silly," Eddie told her. "Your guts are perfectly safe with

meeeeeeeeeeee." With that last word, Eddie started sliding down the steps and landed on a big cardboard box at the bottom of the stairs.

Liza hurried down the steps and touched Eddie's forehead.

"I . . . is he dead?" Melody asked.

"Only in your dreams," Eddie said. The box he was sitting on collapsed more and Eddie landed with a thud on the basement floor.

"It'd take more than falling down the stairs to hurt Eddie's hard head," Howie said.

"Very funny," Eddie said as he climbed out of the crushed cardboard.

"I hope there was nothing important in this box," Liza said. "Mrs. Jeepers might kill us."

"Mrs. Jeepers might kill us anyway," Howie whispered softly under his breath and used his free hand to cover his neck.

"This place is really creepy," Liza said, holding up her candle.

Melody nodded. "If I were a monster, this is exactly where I'd hide out." The four kids looked around the dusty, cobweb-filled basement. Broken chairs and cardboard boxes were stacked all around them.

"This place stinks like Eddie's soccer shirt," Howie complained.

Eddie pulled the mask off his face and glanced around. "I'd sure rather be playing soccer than poking around this hole."

"I don't think anyone's down here," Howie said. "Mrs. Jeepers must be somewhere else."

"But this is the only place we haven't looked," Melody reminded him.

Liza gulped and pointed to a far corner of the basement. "Someone, or something, is down here," she whispered. "Look."

The four kids stared at a green glow in the darkest part of the basement. Then, without any warning, their candles blew out.

13

Lights!

Liza was in mid-scream when Melody grabbed her arm.

"Let's go!" Howie yelled. The four kids raced up the stairs. Liza almost fell backwards when she saw more of the strange green glow. This time the glow was at the top of the steps.

The eerie green glow reminded Liza of monsters' eyes glaring at her through the blackness of the basement. "We're surrounded!" Liza screamed just as the lights flashed on. Liza was partly blinded by the bright light, but there was no doubt about it. Something or someone big was at the top of the stairs.

Liza rubbed her eyes and saw a blur of purple and green. Mrs. Jeepers, their teacher, stood in front of them on the

steps. Mrs. Jeepers smiled her odd little half smile at the kids and gently rubbed her green brooch with two pointy green fingernails.

"Boys and girls, there is no need to be alarmed," Mrs. Jeepers told them in her strange accent. Her green eyes flashed and her green brooch glowed. "I am terribly sorry this storm has frightened you. The timing was most unfortunate."

"We weren't scared," Eddie said quickly. "Liza was just afraid you might be hurt since you disappeared."

Mrs. Jeepers ushered the four kids up the steps and into the dining room. Outside, the storm seemed to be ending. Carey, Huey, and the rest of the third-graders were still huddled together in a corner. They all breathed a sigh of relief when Mrs. Jeepers came into the room with Melody, Howie, Liza, and Eddie.

"That's what we saw in the basement," Howie whispered, pointing to Mrs.

Jeepers. “It was just Mrs. Jeepers' fingernails and brooch glowing in the corner.”

“But we were right beside the steps,” Liza whispered. “She couldn't have beaten us to the top unless. . .”

Melody gasped. “Unless she FLEW!”

“Like a bat,” Howie finished. “A vampire bat!”

“Why did you think I disappeared?” Mrs. Jeepers asked the third-graders. “I was just down in the basement to put in a new fuse.”

Eddie poked his elbow into Liza's side. “She was in the basement all right,” he whispered. “I bet she took a bat-nap in her coffin.”

Liza ignored Eddie and stared at Mrs. Jeepers' fingernails. Liza's face turned pale as Mrs. Jeepers' fingernails glowed an eerie shade of ghoul green.

“Liza,” Mrs. Jeepers said, reaching her glowing green fingernails toward Liza.

"Are you all right? You look somewhat ill."

"I . . . I'm fine," Liza stuttered. "Eddie's story must have scared me more than I thought."

"A scary story?" Mrs. Jeepers asked, touching the green brooch at her neck.

"That reminds me," Melody interrupted. "We saw some very unusual paintings in the hallway when we were looking for you."

"Yeah," Howie said. "They seemed almost lifelike."

Mrs. Jeepers smiled. "Thank you. I try to make my paintings come alive . . . to almost jump off the canvas."

"Oh, they do," Melody said quickly. "But we also found some strange masks. Did you paint those, too?"

Mrs. Jeepers shook her head. "Oh, no. I see you have found my surprise. Those are party favors. Everyone may take one home." Mrs. Jeepers turned to lead

the students to the room with the masks.

"All right!" Eddie said, holding up his mask. Carey took one look at the mask and ran screaming into the corner. Eddie laughed and winked at Melody. "Maybe this wasn't such a bad party after all."

Melody sighed. "This is the perfect party for a monster like Eddie."

"Yeah," Liza said with a giggle, "the first annual Bailey City Monster Bash."

"Oh, no," Howie said, rolling his eyes. "If Mrs. Jeepers stays in Bailey City, we'd better watch out. I have a terrible feeling our monster troubles are just beginning."

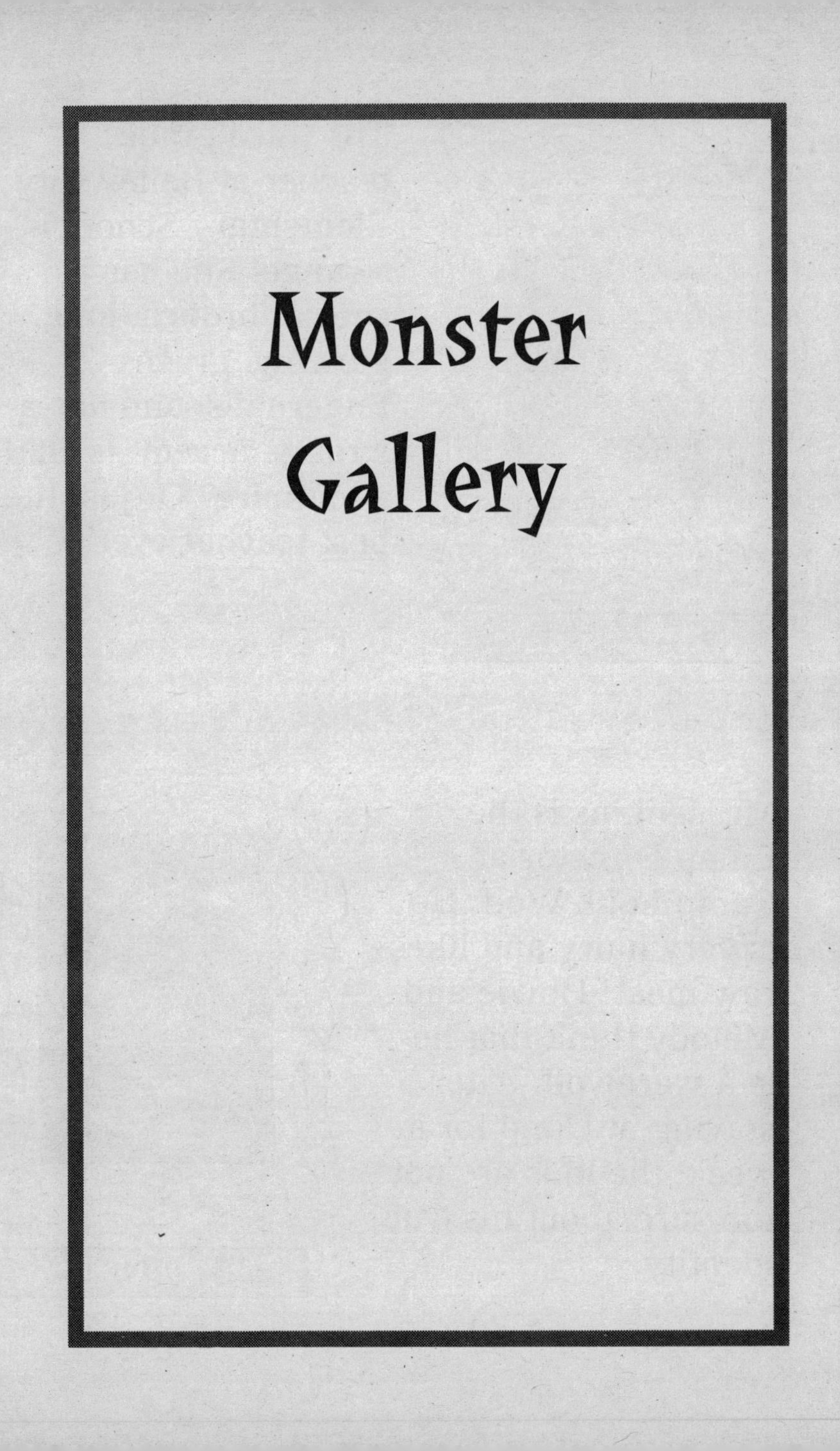

Monster Gallery

The third-grade teacher at Bailey City Elementary School is strange! She has a special brooch, long, glowing, green fingernails, and has a strange accent. Is she a **vampire**? Or just the best teacher ever?

Mr. Jenkins is the Camp Director at Camp Lone Wolf. He is very hairy and likes raw meat! Howie and Melody think that he is a **werewolf**. After staying at camp for a week, the kids are not too sure about his true identity.

• MR. JOLLY •

After the regular janitor leaves Bailey Elementary, Mr. Jolly comes to town. He jingles his keys, keeps the building ice-cold, and writes in a little notebook. Mr. Jolly even has a helper named Eli who has a pointy black beard and dresses all in green! Maybe he really is **Santa Claus**!

Mr. O'Grady thinks that Eddie's jokes are funny. He loves to trick people and Eddie thinks that he has magic stones just like a **leprechaun**. Mr. O'Grady helps out in gym class and teaches the kids a few tricks out on the basketball court.

• MR. O'GRADY •

When Eddie's Aunt Mathilda is sick, the kids visit her. Howie thinks that he sees a man in the attic window—even though Aunt Mathilda lives alone. Maybe there is a **ghost**! Then garlic potato chips are found in the attic. Uncle Jasper's favorite!

On a class trip to the science museum, the kids meet Dr. Victor and his assistant Frank. Liza has just read a book about **Frankenstein** and she thinks Frank is Frankenstein's monster! He is very tall and he looks just like the famous monster!

• FRANK •

Art class in school will never be the same! Mrs. Zork is strangely pale and talks about faraway places. Howie thinks she is an **alien** stealing Bailey City's colors!

By the oak tree in the playground, there is a tiny bottle. Eddie tosses the bottle in the junkyard while Melody wishes someone would clean up the mess. And someone does! Lots of wishes are coming true around Bailey City. Maybe a **genie** has moved in next door.

• CAPTAIN TEACH •

Camp Lone Wolf is a place for some weird people. Maybe even a **pirate** and his parrot. With buried treasure, a map, and swords, who wouldn't believe the boating teacher is a pirate searching for buried treasure?

There is a new gym in Bailey City and everyone wants to take gymnastic classes. The new teacher wears all black, talks in rhyme, and has a black cat. She looks like a **witch** flying through the air when she does flips!

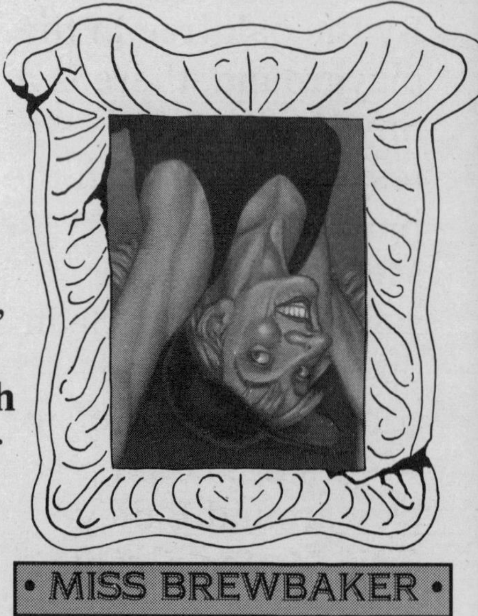

• MISS BREWBAKER •

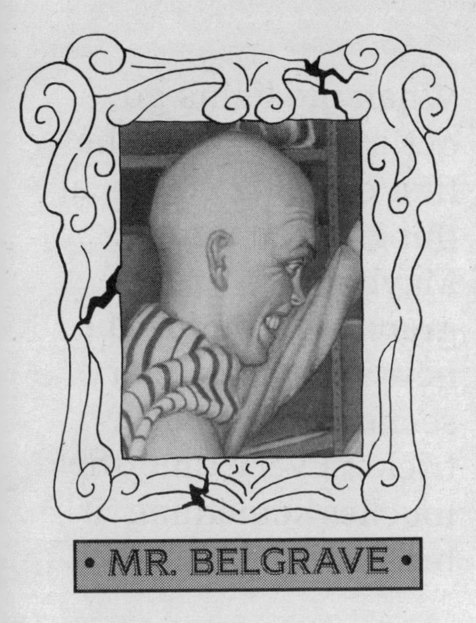

A new band teacher has come to Bailey City to teach music. The very skinny man plays the trumpet and has a strange friend in his room—Claude the **skeleton**! Liza and Eddie think the skeleton is alive!

The cafeteria is decorated for Valentine's Day and there is a new cook. She wears all red, makes special heart-shaped cookies, and has tiny pins to give to everyone. She's a real **cupid**! Even Eddie is being nice to Carey!

• MRS. KIDWELL •

When the lights go out in school, it is the first of many electrical things to go wrong. Maybe there are **gremlins** around. The new school secretary seems up to some tricks! Every time she touches something, it breaks!

The swimming and snorkeling instructor at Camp Lone Wolf is a bit strange. She wears a black wet suit, speaks about a faraway land, and plays the bagpipes! Maybe the rumors that there is a sea **monster** in the lake are true!

• MISS MACFARLAND •

The Bailey Boomers need a new soccer coach. They have not won a soccer game all year. No one is sure where *this* coach came from. She stares off into space all the time—just like a **zombie**!

With his strange accent and his chalky white skin, the new counselor at Bailey City is pretty strange. His hands are ice-cold and he likes to drink pink lemonade all the time. Could there be another **vampire** in Bailey City?

Bell Construction is building a new playground at school. The man in charge wears bright green overalls and boots that have curled-up toes. Are these workers **elves**, creating magic?

After a terrible dust storm, a mysterious woman turns up at school. She has a silver suitcase and the strangest equipment. She is not like other school nurses! She seems like a **Martian**!

The Bailey City library has large **gargoyles** perched on the roof. But there are plans to destroy the library and build a new one! The kids love the gargoyles. Especially one that looks just like the new bus driver!

Having to do a research report at the library is not Eddie's favorite activity. But Mr. Merle, the librarian, has some plans to make the library a magical place. Like a **wizard**, he turns the library into a Reading Kingdom.

The Bailey Batters need help. They want to win the pennant for the season. Coach Tuttle doesn't seem to know much about softball. He knows more about falling down and wrapping limbs! By the end of practice he's wrapped up like a real **mummy**!

Monster-ously Fun Activities and Puzzles!

All About Your Monster Nails

You can have fun with the nails during the day and then watch them glow at night!

For the best glow-in-the-dark nails, keep the nails under a light for about ten minutes (the longer you keep them in the light, the longer the glow will last).

Place each plastic finger on your fingers.

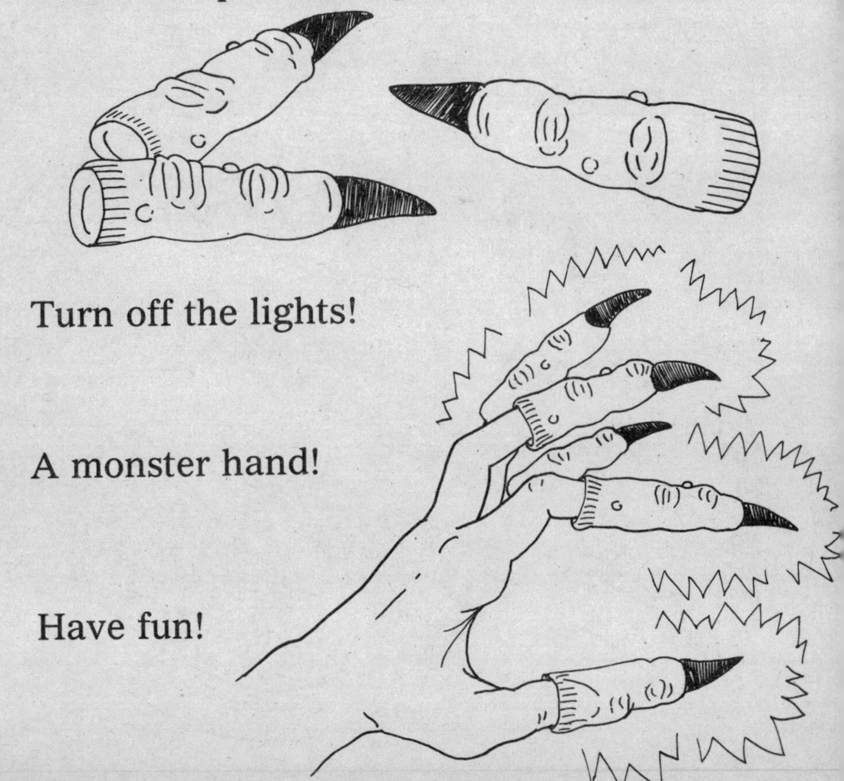

Turn off the lights!

A monster hand!

Have fun!

A Monster Maze

Eddie is meeting his friends at the soccer field. Can you help him find his way there?

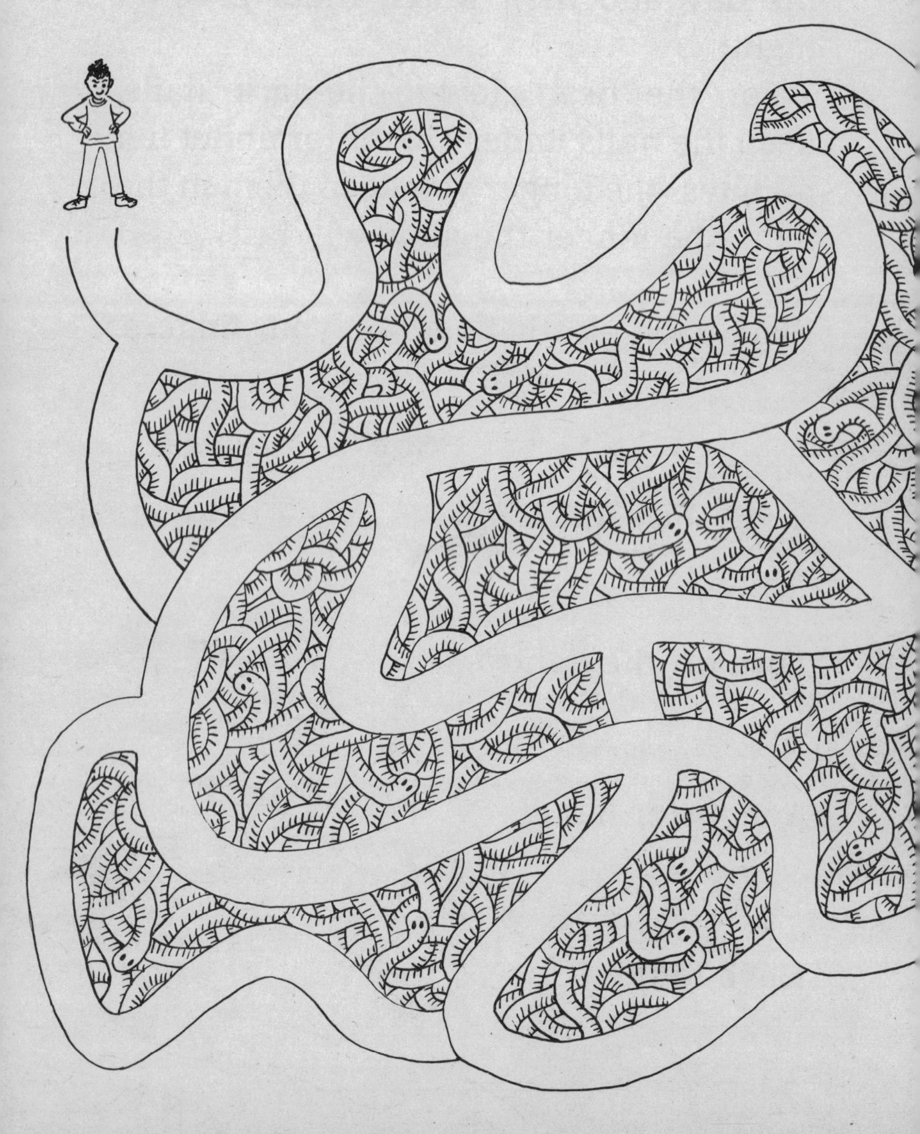

Answer on page 96.

The Great Monster Match!

Can you match up these monsters? Draw a line connecting the grown-up living in Bailey City with the monster that Liza, Howie, Melody, and Eddie believe them to be!

Mr. Belgrave	Mummy
Coach Graves	Skeleton
Miss Brewbaker	Alien
Mr. Jenkins	Gremlin
Coach Tuttle	Zombie
Uncle Jasper	Witch
Mrs. Zork	Werewolf
Mrs. Kidwell	Ghost

Answer on page 96.

Monster Fill-ins

There are pretty weird grown-ups living in Bailey City! Do these pictures look familiar? Fill in the names from the word bank.

1.

Miss ______________________

2.

Mrs. ____________________

3.

4.

Mr. ____________________ Mrs. ____________________

5.

6.

Captain____________________ 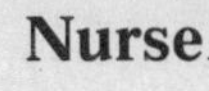 Nurse____________________

7.

Mr. ____________________

Word Bank

Jenkins
MacFarland
Teach
Redding
Rosenbloom
O'Grady
Zork

Answers on page 96.

Eddie's Monster Jokes

Why did the monster cross the road?
Because the chicken was on vacation!

What is a werewolf's favorite snack?
Moon-pie!

What insect isn't dead or alive?
A zom-bee!

What do you call two mummies who live together?
Tomb-mates!

What do ghosts eat for breakfast?
Boo-berry pancakes!

What is Dracula's favorite ice cream?
Vein-illa ice cream!

What kind of music do mummies like best?
Wrap music!

What game do ghosts like to play?
Hide and shriek!

Knock-knock.
Who's there?
Boo.
Boo who?
Don't cry! I'll tell you another joke!

What do you get when you cross a werewolf and an egg?
A very hairy omelette!

Where do ghosts like to swim?
Lake Eerie!

What is a witch's favorite subject in school?
Spelling!

A Monster Puzzle!

Answer the questions by filling in the blanks. You can check your answers when you are done. The answers are printed on page 97. But don't look yet! Try to answer as many as you can. Then try to find the answers in the puzzle. The answers can be horizontal [→], vertical [↑ ↓], diagonal [↗↘], and even backwards!

1. What jewelry does Mrs. Jeepers always wear? __ __ __ __ __ __
2. What instrument does Mr. Belgrave play? __ __ __ __ __ __ __
3. What color is Eddie's hair? __ __ __
4. What creature do the kids think Mrs. Jeepers is? __ __ __ __ __ __ __
5. What is Coach Graves' favorite sport? __ __ __ __ __ __
6. What city do Liza, Melody, Howie, and Eddie live in?

__ __ __ __ __ __ __ __ __ __

7. Which coach in Bailey City likes to wrap things up? __ __ __ __ __ __

8. What animal does the hairy Mr. Jenkins like best? __ __ __ __

9. What funny way does Mrs. Brewbaker talk? __ __ __ __ __

10. This counselor can be a real pain in the neck: Mr. __ __ __ __ __

R	E	D	Q	P	H	F	L	O	W	B	A
A	B	A	I	L	E	Y	C	I	T	Y	Z
D	R	E	A	C	V	A	M	P	I	R	E
O	H	T	R	U	M	D	E	M	A	P	O
N	Y	W	R	B	T	U	T	T	L	E	B
A	M	I	V	U	O	E	D	R	A	J	R
G	E	K	T	H	M	A	R	S	Y	W	O
I	P	A	T	I	N	P	E	F	U	I	O
V	D	R	A	K	E	A	E	J	M	V	C
M	B	D	H	V	A	J	P	T	D	O	H
D	R	E	C	C	O	S	T	S	R	J	E
C	S	K	S	E	G	N	B	J	A	T	Z

Monster Crossword Puzzle

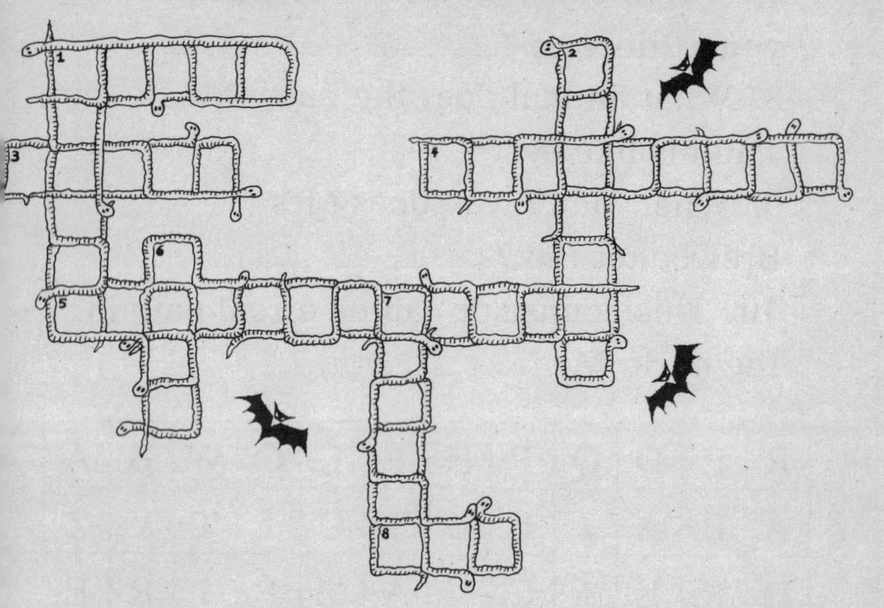

Across

1. Color of Mrs. Jeepers' fingernails
3. Bailey Elementary School's counselor
4. What Mrs. Jeepers likes to wear
5. Where Mrs. Jeepers lives
8. Color of Mrs. Jeepers' hair

Down

1. Howie's favorite flavor potato chips
2. Where the Bailey Kids meet in the schoolyard
6. Where Howie's dad works
7. Melody's favorite sport

Answers on page 97.

Your Own Bailey City Monster!

Here is your chance to come up with your own Bailey School Kids adventure! Fill in the blanks below. Share it with your friends!

There are some pretty weird grown-ups living in Bailey City.

But could the new ____________________

____

who has ______________________________

____

***really* be a __________________________?**

The Bailey School Kids are going to find out!

In the space below, draw the monster who has just moved to Bailey City.

Monster Mush

You will need:

one werewolf brain (one cup peanut butter)
two Martian tongues (two whole peeled bananas)
four ghost hands (four bread slices)
five zombie eyeballs (five red ripe strawberries)

What better snack for a monster party than Monster Mush? Take one cup of peanut butter and put it into a bowl with two whole peeled bananas. With clean hands squish the peanut butter and bananas together. It's messy, but fun. After washing your hands, spread the mixture onto four bread slices with a spoon or dull knife. With a dull knife (or ask for adult help) cut the green tops off five strawberries. Slice the strawberries into sections and lay them on top of the peanut butter and banana mixture. Cut each bread slice into four sections. Now you can enjoy delicious monster mush with all your monster friends.

Cold Brewbaker's Brew

You will need:

six cups Frankenstein sweat (six cups of orange juice)
one big ghost flea (one tablespoon sugar)
four zombie eyeballs (four red ripe strawberries)
one cup ghost blood (one cup milk)

Wash down Monster Mush with a delicious drink of Brewbaker's Brew. (You might just flip over it!) Put sugar in a bowl. Dab a little orange juice on the rims of four glasses. Put the rims of the glasses into the sugar. This is especially fun if you have colored sugar. Then stir the orange juice, milk, and the rest of the sugar together. Put this mixture in the glasses. Push a strawberry onto the rim of each glass. (You might need to make a small slit in each strawberry with a dull knife.) Don't forget to store your brew in the refrigerator or, better yet, drink up!

Note: To make a magical foam mysteriously appear, put the brew in a blender. With an adult's help, blend for thirty seconds. Yummy!

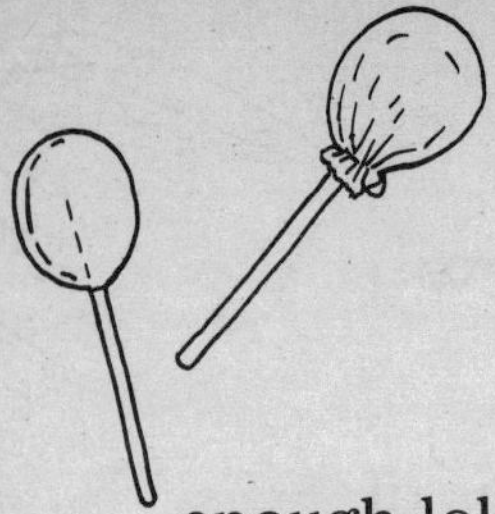

Lollipop Ghosts

You will need:

enough lollipops for all the monsters you know.
one box of tissues
ribbon or colorful string
one black marker

Take two tissues and one lollipop. Place the tissue over the lollipop. Tie ribbon or string around the stick right at the bottom of the lollipop. Use the black marker to draw a ghostly face.

Sweet Spider Treats

Mr. Jenkins loves to eat spiders! But everyone will love these delicious spider treats.

You will need:

four chocolate snack cakes (the rounded kind are best)
twenty-four pieces of black licorice
eight red candies

Stick eight pieces of licorice around the sides of each snack cake. Bend the licorice to look like spider legs. Put two red candies on one end of each cake for eyes. Then offer Sweet Spider Treats to your friends.

Monster Masks

You will need:
plain white paper plates
construction paper
markers or crayons
scissors
glue
yarn or string

Decide what kind of monster face you want to make. Use construction paper, markers, and crayons to draw the monster's face on the paper plate. Ask your mom or dad to help cut out the eyes and to punch a hole on either side of the mask.

Thread two pieces of yarn through the holes and tie a knot.

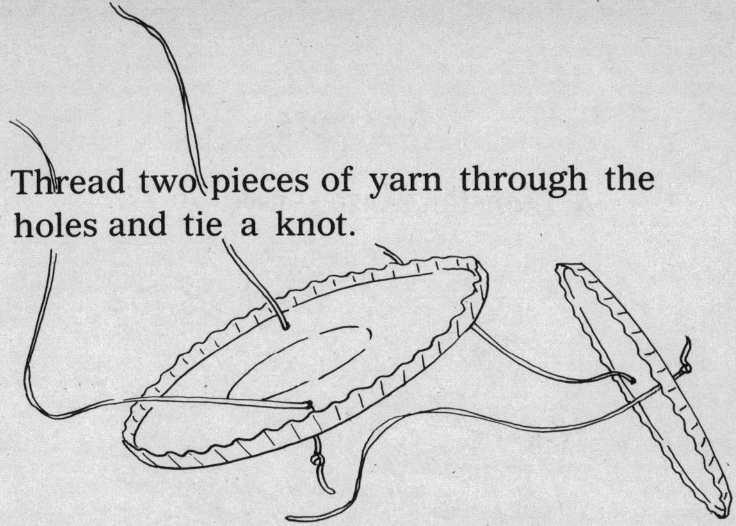

Now you're ready to put your mask on. You and your monster friends can put on a play! But be careful — don't scare any teachers!!!

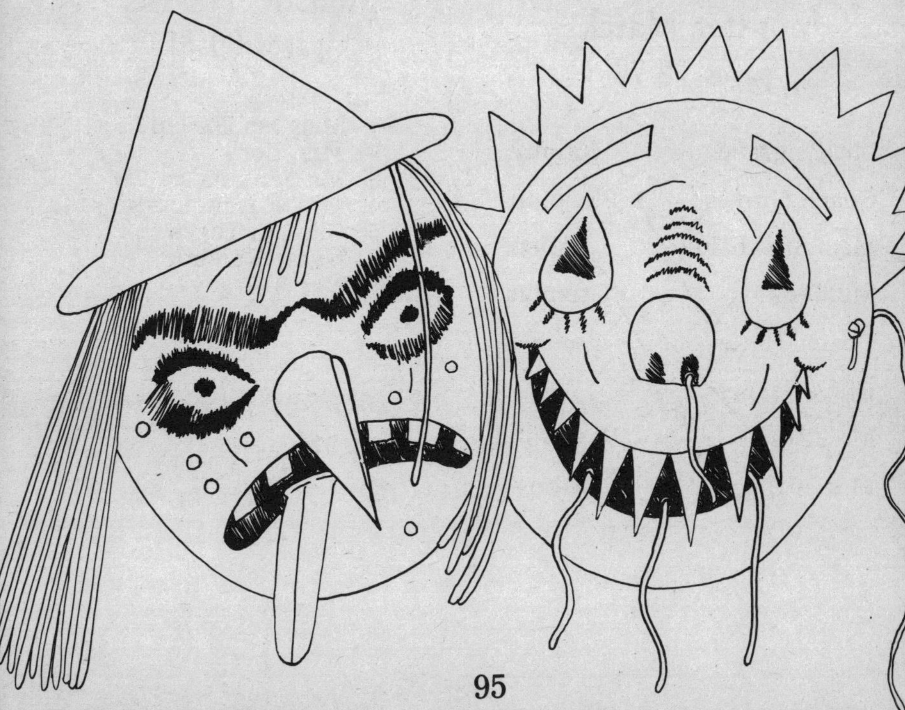

Answers

A Monster Maze—pages 76-77

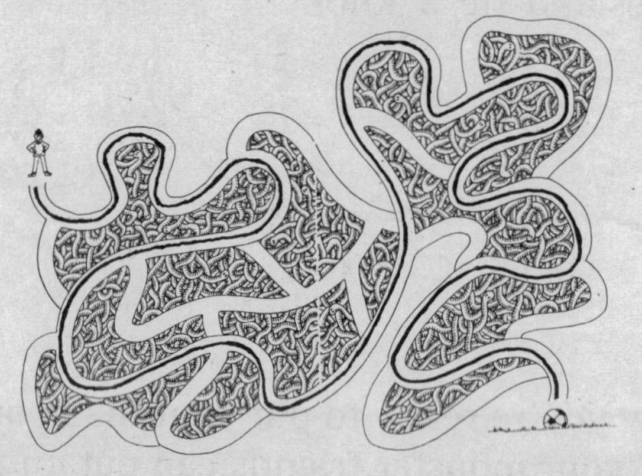

The Great Monster Match! pages 78-79

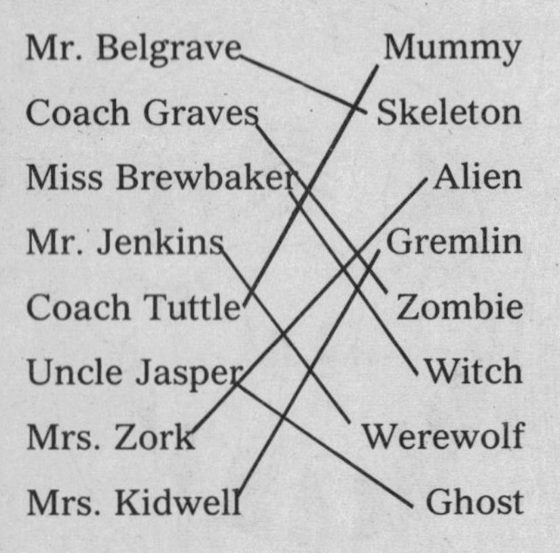

Monster Fill-Ins pages 80-81

1. Miss MacFarland
2. Mrs. Zork
3. Mr. Jenkins
4. Mrs. Rosenbloom
5. Captain Teach
6. Nurse Redding
7. Mr. O'Grady

Answers

A Monster Puzzle—pages 84-85

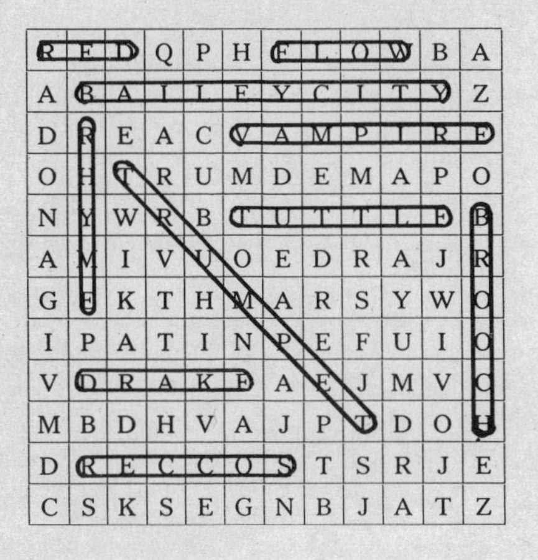

R	E	D	Q	P	H	F	L	O	W	B	A
A	B	A	I	L	E	Y	C	I	T	Y	Z
D	R	E	A	C	V	A	M	P	I	R	E
O	H	T	R	U	M	D	E	M	A	P	O
N	Y	W	R	B	T	U	T	T	L	E	B
A	M	I	V	U	O	E	D	R	A	J	R
G	E	K	T	H	M	A	R	S	Y	W	O
I	P	A	T	I	N	P	E	F	U	I	O
V	D	R	A	K	E	A	E	J	M	V	C
M	B	D	H	V	A	J	P	T	D	O	H
D	R	E	C	C	O	S	T	S	R	J	E
C	S	K	S	E	G	N	B	J	A	T	Z

1. Brooch
2. Trumpet
3. Red
4. Vampire
5. Soccer
6. Bailey City
7. Tuttle
8. Wolf
9. Rhyme
10. Drake

Monster Crossword Puzzle—page 86

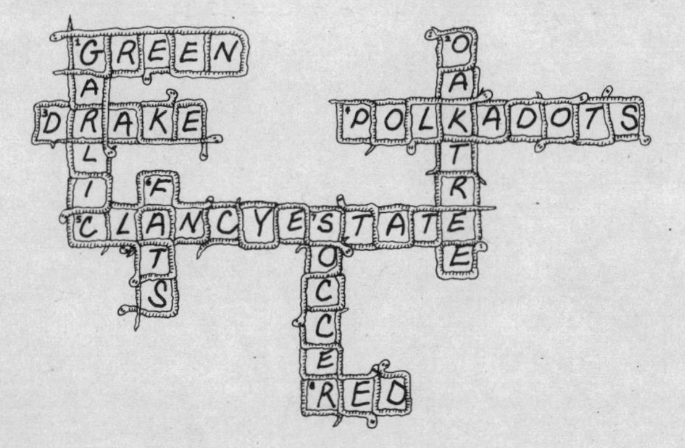

Debbie Dadey and Marcia Thornton Jones have fun writing stories together. When they both worked at an elementary school in Lexington, Kentucky, Debbie was the school librarian and Marcia was a teacher. During their lunch break in the school cafeteria, they came up with the idea of the Bailey School kids.

Recently Debbie and her family moved to Aurora, Illinois. Marcia and her husband still live in Kentucky where she continues to teach. How do these authors still write together? They talk on the phone and use computers and fax machines!

Frankenstein Doesn't Plant Petunias, Ghosts Don't Eat Potato Chips, and Aliens Don't Wear Braces ... or do they?

Find out about the creepiest, weirdest, funniest things that happen to The Bailey School Kids!™ Collect and read them all!

❑ BAS43411-X	Vampires Don't Wear Polka Dots	$2.99
❑ BAS44061-6	Werewolves Don't Go to Summer Camp	$2.99
❑ BAS44477-8	Santa Claus Doesn't Mop Floors	$2.99
❑ BAS44822-6	Leprechauns Don't Play Basketball	$2.99
❑ BAS45854-X	Ghosts Don't Eat Potato Chips	$2.99
❑ BAS47071-X	Frankenstein Doesn't Plant Petunias	$2.99
❑ BAS47070-1	Aliens Don't Wear Braces	$2.99
❑ BAS47297-6	Genies Don't Ride Bicycles	$2.99
❑ BAS47298-4	Pirates Don't Wear Pink Sunglasses	$2.99
❑ BAS48112-6	Witches Don't Do Backflips	$2.99
❑ BAS48113-4	Skeletons Don't Play Tubas	$2.99
❑ BAS48114-2	Cupid Doesn't Flip Hamburgers	$2.99
❑ BAS48115-0	Gremlins Don't Chew Bubble Gum	$2.99
❑ BAS22635-5	Monsters Don't Scuba Dive	$2.99
❑ BAS22636-3	Zombies Don't Play Soccer	$2.99
❑ BAS22638-X	Dracula Doesn't Drink Lemonade	$2.99
❑ BAS22637-1	Elves Don't Wear Hard Hats	$2.99
❑ BAS50960-8	Martians Don't Take Temperatures	$2.99
❑ BAS50961-6	Gargoyles Don't Drive School Buses	$2.99
❑ BAS50962-4	Wizards Don't Need Computers	$2.99
❑ BAS22639-8	Mummies Don't Coach Softball	$2.99
❑ BAS84886-0	Cyclops Doesn't Roller-Skate	$2.99
❑ BAS88134-5	Bailey School Kids Super Special #1 Mrs. Jeepers Is Missing!	$4.99

Available wherever you buy books, or use this order form

Scholastic Inc., P.O. Box 7502, 2931 East McCarty Street, Jefferson City, MO 65102

Please send me the books I have checked above. I am enclosing $_____ (please add $2.00 to cover shipping and handling). Send check or money order — no cash or C.O.D.s please.

Name ______________________________

Address ______________________________

City ______________________ State/Zip ______________

Please allow four to six weeks for delivery. Offer good in the U.S. only. Sorry, mail orders are not available to residents of Canada. Prices subject to change.

BSK396